# Disney's

# ATLANTIS
## THE LOST EMPIRE

W9-BEG-482

# MILO'S STORY

Copyright © 2001 by Disney Enterprises, Inc. All rights reserved under
International and Pan-American Copyright Conventions. Published in the United States
by Random House, Inc., New York, and simultaneously in Canada by Random House of
Canada Limited, Toronto, in conjunction with Disney Enterprises, Inc. RANDOM HOUSE
and colophon are registered trademarks and A STEPPING STONE BOOK and colophon are
trademarks of Random House, Inc.
Library of Congress Card Catalog Number: 00-111943
ISBN: 0-7364-1135-6

Printed in the United States of America
May 2001
10 9 8 7 6 5 4 3 2 1

www.randomhouse.com/kids/disney
www.disneybooks.com

Mr. Whitmore glanced over Milo's shoulder. The ancient drawings and symbols made no sense to him. The Journal was written in a language that no longer existed.

Luckily, Milo was a language expert. He studied languages of all kinds. The Journal *was* hard to decipher, even for him. But he could read it!

"I will find Atlantis!" Milo shouted. "Even if I have to rent a rowboat."

Mr. Whitmore liked Milo's energy. And his determination. But most of all, he liked the fact that Milo could read *The Shepherd's Journal*. Not only that, Milo was very good with maps. He was a cartographer.

"For years your granddad bent my ear

with stories about that old book," Mr. Whitmore said, pointing to the Journal. "I didn't believe him, so I finally made a bet with the old coot. I said, 'Thatch, if you ever actually find that so-called Journal, not only will I finance the expedition, but I'll kiss you full on the mouth.' Imagine my embarrassment when he found the darn thing!"

Milo's jaw dropped. Finding Atlantis would take a lot of work. And a lot of money. "But, Mr. Whitmore, in order to do what you're proposing, you're going to need a crew—"

Mr. Whitmore grinned. "Got 'em all. . . .

the best of the best! All we need now is an expert in gibberish."

Milo looked down at *The Shepherd's Journal*. He had dreamed of finding the ancient book for years. Now here it was— right in his hands. And *he* was going to be part of an expedition to find the lost city!

Milo looked up at the picture of his grandfather hanging on the wall. Finally, he'd have a chance to make Thaddeus Thatch proud!

## Chapter 2

# INTO THE DEEP

The next thing Milo knew, he was out on the ocean with the rest of the expedition crew. The enormous submarine that would take them on their journey was called the *Ulysses*.

Milo walked through the ship. He saw the loading bay and the launch bay. He found a work area and a huge garage filled with vehicles and machinery of all kinds. He overheard a grizzled old cook named Cookie complaining to Helga Sinclair, the second-in-command, about the food that had been packed.

Out of the blue, a siren blared.

"Attention." A scratchy voice echoed over the loudspeaker. It was Mrs. Packard. She was the sub's communications officer. "All hands to the launch bay. Final loading in progress."

Milo was practically run over by a crewmate on his way to the launch bay. It was Vinny Santorini, the guy in charge of explosives. Vinny was hurriedly pushing a large wheelbarrow full of dynamite and other explosives—a *lot* of explosives.

Milo wasn't sure what all the explosives were for. Or all the machinery, for that matter. He was feeling a little dazed when Mr. Whitmore spotted him.

"Milo!" Mr. Whitmore called out. "I want you to meet the leader of the expedition, Commander Rourke."

Rourke held out his hand and smiled. "Pleasure to meet the grandson of ol' Thaddeus. See you got that Journal. Nice pictures, but I prefer a good Western myself."

Milo grinned. As far as he was concerned, the best Western ever written couldn't come close to *The Shepherd's Journal*. It was history. And discovery. And knowledge.

The scratchy voice came over the loudspeaker again. "Attention, all personnel.

Launch will commence in fifteen minutes."

The *Ulysses* stood ready.

Milo waved good-bye to Mr. Whitmore and got into the sub. The door closed behind him with a loud clang.

"Take her down!" Rourke's voice echoed over the loudspeaker.

Outside, Mr. Whitmore crossed his fingers for luck. The sub plunged into the water with a mighty splash. Then it disappeared completely . . . heading into the deep.

Inside the sub, Milo found his cabin. He threw his gear on his bunk and lay down for a quick nap.

But a sudden bright light shining in his face startled him!

"You have disturbed the dirt!" yelled a short, strange-looking man named Molière. He pushed Milo off the bunk and pulled back the sheet.

Underneath were small piles of dirt. Each

pile was marked with a flag from a different country. "Dirt from around the globe!" the funny man said. "Spanning the centuries!"

The man grabbed Milo's hands. With a pair of tweezers he pulled a speck of dirt from under one of Milo's fingernails. Then he held a high-powered magnifying lens in front of his eyes. "Lead from the pencil—you chew the eraser; ham sandwich—no mayo; I see you have a cat; mold spores from Mesopotamian parchment circa 2000 B.C.," he rattled off. "These are all the microscopic fingerprints of the mapmaker."

Milo was amazed. Molière knew all about him from one tiny piece of dirt!

Then, suddenly, Molière remembered his

messed-up dirt piles. "This is an outrage! You must leave at once! Out!"

He pushed Milo out the door—straight into Joshua Sweet, the sub's doctor. Sweet stuck a thermometer in Milo's mouth.

"Milo Thatch? You're my three o'clock," he explained. "Well—no time like the present!"

Sweet chattered away while he gave Milo a physical—right then and there. But before Sweet could finish, Milo was called to the bridge to give a presentation to the rest of the crew.

Milo was the only crew member who could read *The Shepherd's Journal*. It was his job to tell the others what to expect on the journey. It wouldn't be easy.

Luckily, Milo had slides to help with his presentation. He flashed a picture of a huge, lobster-like sea creature. "This is an illustration of the Leviathan—the creature guarding the entrance to Atlantis," he said.

The Leviathan was big and scary-looking. Myths told of sailors going crazy just from looking at it. But the crew seemed unimpressed.

"So we find this masterpiece—then what?" Rourke wanted to know.

Milo cleared his throat as he forwarded to the next slide—a route to Atlantis. "You see, according to the Journal, the path to Atlantis will take us down a tunnel at the bottom of the ocean. And we'll come up a curve, into an air pocket, right here, where we'll find the remnants of an ancient highway that will lead us to Atlantis—kind of like the grease trap in your sink."

Audrey Ramirez, the crew's young mechanic, looked bored.

Suddenly one of the sub's officers called to the captain. "You'd better come look at this, sir!"

"Okay, class dismissed. Give me exterior lights," Rourke ordered.

Mrs. Packard pulled off her headphones. "Commander, I think you should hear this," she said in her raspy voice.

Mrs. Packard flipped a switch. A strange metallic sound echoed over the ship's speakers.

"What is it?" Rourke asked. "A pod of whales?"

"Nah." Mrs. Packard shook her head. "Bigger."

The noise got louder and louder and then stopped. Everyone was breathing a sigh of relief when—

*Slam!* Something huge hit the ship.

Outside, a humongous lobster-like creature was attacking the sub. It was the Leviathan! It batted the ship around with a single claw. Then it closed in. . . .

Milo stared at the Leviathan through a window. "Jiminy Christmas!" he yelled. "It's a *machine*!"

Crew members rushed to prepare for battle. But the Leviathan seemed unstoppable. It grabbed the sub and started to crush it.

Tiny subpods zoomed out of the *Ulysses* and launched torpedoes at the Leviathan. It dropped the sub. But a second later, the Leviathan fired an electric beam that melted a hole in the side of the ship.

Water rushed in. The crew was going to drown!

"All hands abandon ship!" Mrs. Packard called over the loudspeaker.

Water was everywhere. Lights flashed. Smoke billowed. Milo followed some of the others to an aqua-evac vehicle and climbed in.

"Lieutenant, get us out of here!" Rourke ordered. But the release lever was jammed. Helga pushed and pulled. Nothing happened.

The Leviathan continued to crush the sub's hull in its huge claws. Time was running out!

Helga gave the lever a final kick.

The exit bay opened. More subpods and three aqua-evacs shot into the ocean just as the mechanical sea monster destroyed the *Ulysses*.

"Where to, Mr. Thatch?" Rourke asked.

"We're looking for a big crevice of some kind!" Milo shouted.

A gaping hole came into view.

"There!" Rourke yelled. "Up ahead!"

Pieces of the crushed sub swirled in the water. The Leviathan closed in. It blasted two of the escape vehicles with its laser.

Milo closed his eyes as his aqua-evac zoomed into the crevice.

## Chapter 3

# THE ROAD TO ATLANTIS

Before long the survivors surfaced in an underground cave. They were exhausted and worried. They'd started their adventure with two hundred crew members. Fewer than twenty were left.

"We have a crisis on our hands," Rourke announced. Helga nodded.

Rourke looked straight at Milo. "Looks like all our chances of survival rest with you," he said. "You and that little book."

Milo noticed that the rest of the crew

looked doubtful. And inside, *he* felt doubtful. Could he do it? He wasn't sure.

The next few hours didn't reassure anyone. First they unloaded all their vehicles from the only remaining aqua-evac. Everyone was assigned a truck to drive. But Milo didn't even know how! (He'd driven a car before—but it was a *bumper* car at Coney Island!)

The crew gave Milo a look of disgust as his truck was hooked to the back of Molière's digger.

Later, after examining a page of the Journal, Milo led the crew through a skull-shaped cave entrance. They barely escaped the giant cave beast that chased them out!

The crew glared at him. Milo gulped—
and turned the Journal right side up. Things
were *not* looking good.

Later on, the crew set up camp in a cave.
A huge glowing rock hung from the ceiling.

Milo pored over the pages of the Journal.
"It just doesn't make sense . . . ," he
muttered to himself.

In one section of the Journal, the shepherd
described something that could be very
important. It was called the Heart of Atlantis.
It seemed to be some kind of power source.

But then, all of a sudden, the Journal
entry just ended. "It's almost like there's a
missing page," Milo said, frowning.

"Kid, relax," Vinny said. "We don't get paid overtime."

Milo nodded. He was tired, and it was time to turn in. He climbed into his drooping tent—he had put it up all by himself—and snuggled into his sleeping bag.

With his tent flap open, he could see the glowing rock hanging from the cave's ceiling. He gazed at it while he thought about the strange entry in the Journal.

Was there a missing page? And if there was, what did it say?

An image of his grandfather flashed into his head. Had his grandfather known about the Heart of Atlantis? What could he tell Milo if he were here? These questions continued to trouble Milo as he fell asleep.

In the middle of the night, Milo woke up and stumbled out of his tent. He heard Mrs. Packard snoring and Cookie mumbling in his sleep.

As Milo passed Rourke's tent, he accidentally shined his flashlight on the glowing rock on the ceiling.

Glittering fireflies suddenly swarmed from the rock! They showered the camp like sparks. Anything they touched instantly burst into flames.

Suddenly the entire camp was on fire!

"Fire! Fire!" Milo shouted.

Everyone awoke with a jolt.

"Get us into those caves!" Rourke ordered. "Move it!"

But to get to the caves, the crew had to cross a nearby bridge.

Halfway across, the fireflies ignited the fuel truck. It exploded in a giant ball of fire.

The explosion broke the bridge in two.

The next thing Milo knew, the vehicles were sliding backward into a giant chasm.

Everyone panicked. And then everything went black.

## Chapter 4

# OUT OF THE FRYING PAN, INTO THE FIRE

"All right, who's not dead? Sound off!" Rourke ordered.

Each crew member moaned in response. Everyone was accounted for . . . except Milo.

Far from the other members of the crew, Milo lay unconscious on a bed of soft volcanic ash. Hovering over him in the darkness were three strangers. They wore masks and carried the spears of warriors.

"He's dressed so strangely," one figure said in his language.

"He must be from the surface," said the small group's leader.

"Should we kill him?" a third warrior asked.

"No," said the leader. "He doesn't appear to be hostile."

One of the warriors touched Milo's eyeglasses with a spear. Milo opened his eyes.

Surprised, Milo tried to sit up. But a sharp pain seared through his shoulder. Touching it gingerly, he felt warm blood.

"Ahhh!" he moaned.

The leader pulled off the mask. Milo

was surprised to see the warrior was a young woman!

Milo and the woman stared at each other for a moment. Then he watched as she held up a piece of blue crystal that hung from her neck. She placed the crystal against Milo's wounded shoulder.

At first Milo wanted to pull away. But something held him there. All of a sudden he felt a tingling sensation run down his arm. When the warrior removed the crystal, his wound was healed!

Milo stood up and swung his arm in a circle. There was no pain! It didn't seem possible.

Milo looked at the compassionate warrior. She was smiling at him. He smiled back. Somehow, in this strange place, it *was* possible.

A million questions raced through Milo's mind. But before he could speak, the roar of his crew's vehicles echoed in the hollow volcano. The three warriors scattered.

"Whoa!" Milo cried. "Wait just a minute! Who are you? Come back!"

Milo chased them over rocks and boulders, but the warriors were too fast. In moments they were gone.

Milo was disappointed. For the first time he wished he were in Atlantis by himself.

Except he wouldn't *really* be by himself. There were other beings living down here— intelligent beings with magic crystals.

Milo's adventure was getting more interesting by the minute. He couldn't wait to see what would happen next!

## Chapter 5

# KING OF ATLANTIS

"Sweet mother of Jefferson Davis!" Cookie exclaimed.

"It's beautiful," Audrey said.

"Milo, I gotta hand it to you," Sweet said. "You really came through."

Milo was stunned. He and the crew stood on a high ledge and looked out over Atlantis. The city was the most magnificent thing he'd ever seen.

But before he could even speak, the Atlantean warriors ambushed the crew.

"Holy cats!" Rourke bellowed. "Who are these guys?"

"They have to be Atlanteans," Milo replied.

"What?" Helga said. "That's impossible!"

One of the warriors stepped forward. "Who are you strangers and where are you from?" she asked in her native language.

"I think it's talking to you," Mole told Milo.

Milo slowly repeated what the young woman had said.

The warrior took off her mask. Milo saw that it was the woman who had healed his shoulder. He felt a little relieved.

"Your manner of speech is strange to me," the warrior said in Atlantean.

Milo tried to say a few more phrases in

Atlantean. They were a little mixed up.

"I travel, friend," he said in Atlantean.

"You are friendly traveler," the warrior replied.

Then Milo had an idea. He asked the warrior if she spoke French. She did!

The other warriors started greeting the crew in languages from around the world! They spoke Italian, Hebrew, French, Greek, German, Chinese, and English!

"We are explorers from the surface world," Rourke told the warriors. "We come in peace."

The lead warrior bowed. "Welcome to the city of Atlantis. Come. You must speak with my father."

The warriors led the crew to the throne room of the Atlantean palace. Then the leader, Kida, introduced the visitors to her father, King Kashekim Nedakh.

"Greetings, Your Highness," she said in Atlantean. "I have brought the visitors."

The king glared at the crew and then replied to his daughter in Atlantean. "You know the law, Kida," he scolded her. "No outsiders may see the city and live."

Kida stood firm before her father. "These people may be able to help us," she argued.

The king shook his head. "We do not need their help."

No one in the crew except Milo understood what the king and his daughter were saying. Milo was taking notes. He could tell that something was wrong. The warrior and her father did not agree.

Rourke cleared his throat. "Your Majesty," he began. "On behalf of my crew, may I say it is an honor to be welcomed to your city?"

"You presume much to think you are welcome here," the king said.

"Sir, we have come a long way looking for—"

"I know what you seek," the king said fiercely. "And you will not find it here. Your journey has been in vain." When Rourke objected, the king added, "You must leave Atlantis at once."

Milo saw Rourke scowl. He hoped Rourke would not show his anger. The king could easily imprison or kill the entire crew!

"May I respectfully request that we stay one night, sir?" Rourke asked. "My men are exhausted. A night would give us time to rest, resupply, and be ready to travel by morning."

The king thought about this request for a long moment. "Very well," he finally said. "One night. That is all."

Milo breathed a sigh of relief. He snapped his notebook shut and followed the rest of the crew out of the throne room.

Something still nagged at him. Kida obviously wanted them to stay. Why? And why did the king want them to leave so badly? What was he afraid of?

Milo suspected that the king was hiding something. But what?

## Chapter 6

# TELL ME MORE

It wasn't long before Milo decided that the best way to find out what was going on was to talk to Kida. So he sneaked back to the palace to wait for her.

Milo hid behind a column. He wanted to see Kida before she saw him. While he was standing there, he practiced what he wanted to say.

"Look, I have some questions for you, and I'm not leaving this city until they're answered," he said out loud to himself.

Then, all of a sudden, someone's hand was covering his mouth. A woman's voice whispered in his ear almost the same words he had just spoken. "I have some questions for you, and you are not leaving the city until they are answered."

For a second Milo was afraid. Then he realized that it was Kida. "Yeah, well, I . . . okay," he stammered.

Kida put a finger to her lips. "Shhh!" she ordered. "Come with me."

She grabbed Milo's arm and led him out of the palace. She took him to a secret cavern. Inside were old tools and statues. Milo was impressed with the Atlantean artifacts.

"There is so much to ask about your world," Kida said. "You are a scholar, are you not? What is your country of origin? When did the floodwaters recede? How did you—"

"Wait a minute!" Milo cried out. "I've got a few questions for you, too."

Milo and Kida took turns asking each other questions. Kida explained that the gods had flooded Atlantis over four thousand years before.

"All I can remember is the sky going dark and people shouting and running. Then a bright light, like a star, floating above the city. My father said it called my mother to it. . . . I never saw her again."

"I'm sorry," Milo said awkwardly.

Then it was Milo's turn. He showed Kida *The Shepherd's Journal*. Kida was amazed to see it. And even more amazed that Milo knew how to read it.

Kida explained to Milo that after the Great Flood, the Atlanteans had lost their knowledge of reading and writing. Their great civilization was steadily crumbling around them.

Kida looked sad for a moment. Then she brightened and stood up. "Here, let me show you something!"

She pulled back a large tarp. Underneath was a giant stone fish.

"It looks like some sort of vehicle," Milo said.

Kida nodded and explained that she had never been able to get it started. But Milo was already examining the fish carefully. Instructions were carved on it.

"Place crystal into slot," he read. "Gently place your hand on the inscription pad."

"Yes," Kida replied.

"Okay, did you turn the crystal one quarter turn back?" Milo asked.

"Yes, yes."

"While your hand was on the inscription pad?"

"No," Kida admitted.

"Oh, well, there's your problem right there," Milo said excitedly. "Okay, give it a try."

Kida completed each step in turn. Suddenly a burst of blue energy lit up the fish's surface. There was a tiny shudder, and the fish rose off the ground!

Kida shrieked excitedly.

"You got that right!" Milo agreed. "With this thing, I can see the whole city in no time at all. I wonder how fast it goes?"

Milo put his hand on the fish—and it took off out of control! Milo and Kida dove for cover just as the fish skimmed over their heads and buried itself in the sand.

Milo sat up and shrugged. "So . . . ," he said, feeling a little embarrassed, "who's hungry?"

Milo and Kida decided it was safer to *walk* through the city. Soon they were climbing a giant Atlantean statue. When they got to the top, Milo's eyes widened in awe as he looked out over the lost city of Atlantis once again.

"My grandpa used to tell me stories of

this place as far back as I can remember," he explained as he wiped a tear from his cheek. "I just wish he could be standing here with me."

Kida nodded. She seemed to be listening carefully.

Milo touched Kida's arm. They came from different worlds, but in many ways, they were very much alike.

## Chapter 7

# HEART OF ATLANTIS

After a long day of exploring, Kida led Milo to a small pool at the edge of the city. He noticed that there were steps leading down to the water.

"You know, Kida, the most we ever hoped to find was some crumbling buildings, maybe some broken pottery," he said. "Instead we find a living, thriving society."

Kida shook her head. "We are *not* thriving. True, our people live, but our culture is dying. We are like a stone the ocean beats against—with each passing year a little more of us is worn away."

"I wish there was something I could do," Milo said.

"That is why I have brought you here," Kida replied. "You do swim, do you not?"

Milo felt a little nervous. He *did* swim— about as well as he drove.

"I swim pretty good," he finally said. He puffed up his chest. "Hey, you're talking to the belly flop champ at Camp Runamuk."

Kida dove into the water. Milo followed. They swam through the flooded ruins of Atlantean buildings.

Milo kept waiting for Kida to go up to the surface for air. But she just kept swimming.

Finally, when his lungs were about to burst, they reached a small air pocket.

Gasping for air, Milo bumped his head on the ceiling. He could have drowned! But in no time, Kida took another deep breath and went back under. Milo followed, and this time the journey was much shorter. Kida pointed to an underwater mural. Milo swam closer and started to read the symbols. Excited, he motioned for her to go back up for air.

"This is amazing!" he shouted. "A complete history of Atlantis!"

Kida's eyes widened. "The light I saw— the star in the middle of the city. What does the writing say about that?" she asked.

"It's the Heart of Atlantis!" Milo said. "That's what the shepherd was talking about. It wasn't a star. It was—it was some kind of crystal." He pointed to the crystal around Kida's neck. "Like these!"

All at once, Milo understood. There *was* a page missing from the Journal. And he was sure that page was all about the Heart of Atlantis!

"The power source I've been looking for and the bright light you remember. They're the same thing. It's what's keeping all of these things . . . you . . . all of Atlantis— alive!"

Kida looked very doubtful. "Then where is it now?" she asked.

"I don't know." Milo admitted, thinking about the missing Journal page.

Excited, Milo and Kida swam back to the pool. They were greeted by Rourke and the rest of the explorers. At first Milo was glad to see them. Then he noticed the weapons they were holding.

"I'm such an idiot!" Milo smacked his forehead. "This is just another treasure hunt for you," he said to Rourke. "You're after the Crystal!"

Rourke grinned and pulled the missing Journal page from his boot. "You led us right to the treasure chest," he said with a nasty smirk.

One of Rourke's troopers grabbed Kida by the hair. She put up a good fight, but she was quickly outnumbered.

"You don't know what you're tampering with, Rourke," Milo warned.

Rourke didn't seem to be listening. "What's to know? It's big, it's shiny. It's going to make us all rich!"

"You think it's some kind of diamond.

I thought it was some kind of battery. But we're both wrong. It's their life force," Milo explained. "That crystal is the only thing keeping these people alive. You take that away and they'll die."

But Rourke was determined to get the Heart of Atlantis, no matter what the cost. He dragged Milo and Kida back to the palace to search for it.

Inside the throne room, Rourke spotted a lovely reflecting pool. In the middle was a small pile of rocks that formed the Atlantean letter *A*. It looked just like the letter on the cover of *The Shepherd's Journal*.

Rourke stepped into the pool. The water started to vibrate. Moments later Rourke,

Kida, Milo, and Helga slowly began dropping to a lower level. The pool was an aquavator!

Stepping off the aquavator, Milo gaped at what he saw. Hanging above another pool of water was a giant crystal.

It was the Heart of Atlantis. Huge carved figures circled it in midair.

Rourke beamed. "Jackpot," he said.

Kida dropped to her knees. "The kings of our past," she said, overwhelmed.

Suddenly the Crystal began to send out search beams. It homed in on Kida. She froze, as if she were caught in a spell. Her crystal necklace began to float.

In a trance, Kida walked under the

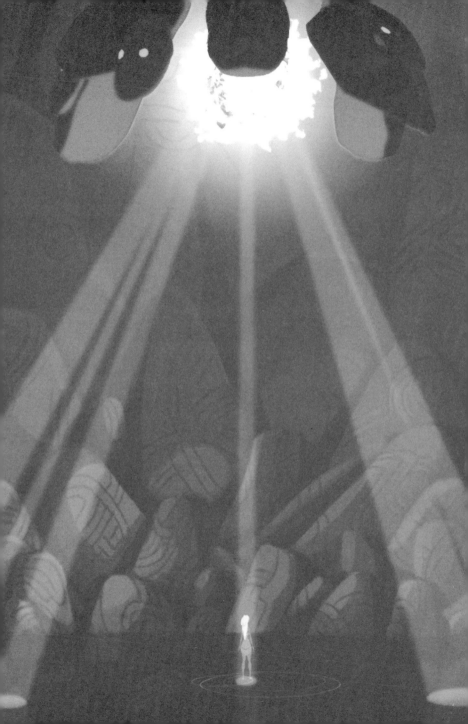

Crystal. She stepped into the pool. The stone guardians around the Crystal moved aside. Another beam of light shone down on her and lifted her into the air. Then the stones surrounded her. Kida had become part of the Heart of Atlantis. She was crystallized!

As soon as the crystallized Kida floated back down to the water, Helga and Rourke grabbed her. They left the chamber and returned to the others, who put Kida into a transport pod. Several troopers guarded their vehicles.

Desperate, Milo turned to each of the crew members. He begged them to think about what was happening. At first they didn't want to hear it—but deep down, they knew that what they were doing was wrong.

Audrey was the first to walk to Milo's side. Then Vinny and Mole. Then Cookie. Mrs. Packard was last.

Milo felt his heart lift. Things were bad, but at least he wasn't alone.

## Chapter 3

# UP, UP, AND AWAY!

Milo's optimism didn't last long. Rourke and Helga still had Kida. Before anyone could stop them, Rourke gunned his engine and took off.

As Rourke led his crew away, the lights in Atlantis flickered and dimmed. The city was already losing its power.

It was time to talk to the king. Milo headed into the throne room. The king of Atlantis was very sick. Sweet had examined the old man. He told Milo there was no hope for him.

Milo stood over the king. "The crystals," he began. "They have some sort of healing energy!"

But the king refused treatment. He was ready to die. Before he did, he begged Milo to help Atlantis. He explained how he had once misused the Crystal.

"I sought to use it as a weapon of war, but its power proved too great to control. It overwhelmed us and led to our destruction." He handed his crystal necklace to Milo. "Return the Crystal. Save the city. Save my daughter." Then the once-great king closed his eyes forever.

Guilt weighed down Milo's heart. The king was dead. The king's daughter—along with the Heart of Atlantis—was being taken to the surface. There was no hope. And it was all his fault.

Sweet interrupted Milo's miserable thoughts. "So, what's it gonna be?" he asked.

Milo was confused. "Excuse me?"

"It's been my experience," Sweet explained to Milo, "when you hit bottom, the

only place left to go is up."

"Who told you that?" Milo asked.

"Fella by the name of Thaddeus Thatch," Sweet answered.

Suddenly Milo wondered what his grandfather would do in this situation. One thing was for sure. He would *not* give up!

Milo smiled. He knew what he had to do. He had to go after Rourke.

Milo raced out of the palace. The other crew members and several Atlantean warriors followed. When they reached Kida's secret cavern, Milo climbed onto one of the stone fish.

"Milo, what do you think you're doing?" Audrey asked.

Milo placed the king's crystal in the slot. "Just follow my lead!" he replied.

Milo started up the fish, then showed everyone else how to get their fish going.

"Saddle up, partners!" Cookie said excitedly.

"All right, this is it! We're gonna rescue the princess. We're gonna save Atlantis. Or we're gonna die trying," Milo declared. The Atlantean armada lifted into the sky. "Now, let's do it!"

Meanwhile, Rourke was escaping with Helga and the crystallized Kida in a gyro-evac hot-air balloon! It floated slowly up the shaft of a volcano.

Milo's crew zoomed in from behind.

"We've got company!" Rourke shouted. "Take her up!"

Vinny activated his fish's lightning blaster. A laser beam shot out from the fish's mouth. It scattered several of Rourke's troopers!

"Okay, now things are getting good!" Vinny shouted.

Sweet and Audrey steered their fish right up to the balloon. The pod containing the crystallized princess was attached to the balloon with chains.

Sweet whipped out his powerful doctor's saw. He and Audrey got to work trying to saw the chains to free the pod.

Milo zoomed by and leaped onto the

balloon. His fish kept flying without him and ripped a hole in the fabric of the gyro-evac balloon!

*Hissssss!* Air began to escape.

"We're losing altitude!" Rourke shouted.

Helga began to throw things overboard to lighten the load. Then Rourke caught her by surprise and threw *her* overboard.

But Rourke didn't see Milo swing forward.

Milo landed right on top of him. Rourke was getting ready to punch Milo when—

*Boom!* Helga fired her flare gun from below. The balloon took a big hit. It was going down.

Rourke was furious. He swung at Milo again, breaking some glass on Kida's pod.

Milo acted fast. He grabbed a shard of crystal-energized glass and cut Rourke's arm with it. In seconds, Rourke began to crystallize—first his arms and then his whole body! After becoming blue like Kida, he became fiery red. Then Rourke changed to black. Finally, he hardened like a burned piece of wood and shattered into tiny pieces.

All of a sudden, the chains that Sweet and Audrey had weakened with the saw broke free. Milo looked down and realized the balloon was about to crash on the princess pod.

At the last second, Milo leaped off the balloon and pushed the pod out of the way. The gyro-evac balloon crashed into the ground and exploded!

Milo heaved a sigh of relief. Rourke was gone for good.

But Milo's troubles were still not over. The exploding balloon had triggered the volcano. Tiny cracks suddenly appeared in the cavern floor. Red-hot lava started to ooze out. The volcano was about to erupt!

"If we don't get out of here, we'll die!" Audrey cried.

Milo was not leaving without Kida. He had to get her back to Atlantis. It was the only way to save the princess and her city!

Milo grabbed a chain and hooked it to the pod. Audrey and Vinny attached the other end to a stone fish. When they took off, the chain snapped!

The lava was getting closer!

Milo leaped off the fish. Dodging the scorching lava, he reattached the chain. "Go!" he shouted.

Vinny gunned the fish's engine just as

the lava touched the bottom of the fish. Escaping at the last second, they raced back to the city.

Outside the palace, the crystallized Kida was reunited with the statues of past kings.

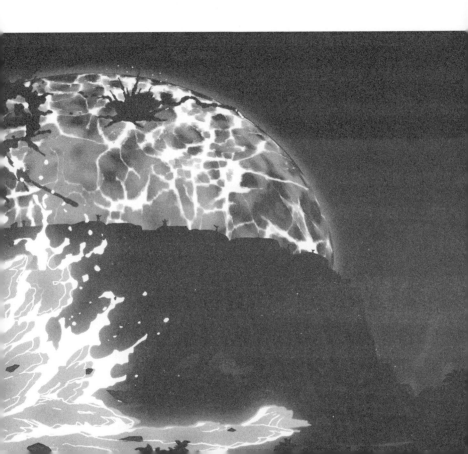

Together they created a powerful force field that protected Atlantis from the volcano's lava.

The lava cooled and hardened above the city. Then it quickly cracked and fell away, leaving a beautiful, thriving Atlantis.

Now that the ancient city had been restored, the Crystal returned Kida to her human form. Milo was overcome with joy and relief. And the princess was equally happy to see the stranger who was now her friend—and a hero!

## Chapter 9

# A NEW BEGINNING

Before long, it was time for Milo's crew to head back to the surface.

To show her gratitude, Kida gave them jewels and treasures. "Atlantis will honor your names forever," she promised.

Vinny was a little embarrassed. "Aw, you know . . . ," he stammered.

"We're really going to miss you," Audrey told Milo.

"Are you sure you want to stay?" Sweet asked Milo. "There's a hero's welcome waiting for the man who discovered Atlantis."

Milo shook his head. "I don't think the world needs another hero," he said. "Besides, I hear there's an opening down here for an expert in gibberish." He pointed to *The Shepherd's Journal*.

Everyone smiled. The world on the surface would not be the same without Milo Thatch.

As Milo and Kida watched everyone depart, Milo thought about what the crew and Mr. Whitmore would say to the rest of the world.

Vinny would talk only about the rocks and little fish they had found. Cookie would report that Helga was missing. Sweet would swear that Rourke had had a nervous breakdown and that he'd just gone to pieces.

Finally, Audrey would declare that Milo had gone down with the sub. . . .

Which was true—except that Milo was still alive and well. In fact, he was happier than he'd ever been in his life. He had new friends and a new home. He had Atlantis.

Milo Thatch, linguist and cartographer— and explorer—was ready for whatever adventures his new life would bring.